Pony Swim

Read all of
MARGUERITE HENRY'S Misty Inn
books!

#1 Welcome Home!
#2 Buttercup Mystery
#3 Runaway Pony
#4 Finding Luck
#5 A Forever Friend
#6 Pony Swim

And coming soon:

#7 Teacher's Pet

MARGUERITE HENRY'S Misty Inn

Pony Swim

By Judy Katschke

Illustrated by Serena Geddes

ALADDIN

New York London Toronto Sydney New Delhi

ALADDIN

An imprint of Simon & Schuster Children's Publishing Division

1230 Avenue of the Americas, New York, New York 10020

First Aladdin paperback edition March 2017

Text copyright © 2017 by The Estate of Marguerite Henry

Illustrations copyright © 2017 by Serena Geddes

Also available in an Aladdin hardcover edition.

All rights reserved, including the right of reproduction in whole or in part in any form.

ALADDIN and related logo are registered trademarks of Simon & Schuster, Inc.

For information about special discounts for bulk purchases, please contact Simon & Schuster Special Sales at 1-866-506-1949 or business@simonandschuster.com.

The Simon & Schuster Speakers Bureau can bring authors to your live event. For more information or to book an event contact the Simon & Schuster Speakers Bureau at 1-866-248-3049 or visit our website at www.simonspeakers.com.

Book designed by Laura Lyn DiSiena

The text of this book was set in Century Expanded.

Manufactured in the United States of America 0217 OFF

10 9 8 7 6 5 4 3 2 1

Library of Congress Control Number 2016954049

ISBN 978-1-4814-6989-0 (hc)

ISBN 978-1-4814-6988-3 (pbk)

ISBN 978-1-4814-6990-6 (eBook)

For Evan, Katie, and Sean

Pony Swim

Chapter 1

TEN-YEAR-OLD WILLA DUNLAP BLINKED HER eyes, once, twice, three times. Was she really seeing what she thought she was seeing?

"Wow, Ben," Willa said to her younger brother. "I've never seen so many people on our beach!"

Willa and Ben stood together on the shore gazing out at the ocean. Next to Willa, nibbling on a clump of marsh grass, was their gentle buckskin mare, Starbuck.

"It may be filled with people now," Ben told his sister. "But in just a few days it will be filled with—"

"Ponies!" Willa cut in excitedly.

Willa and Ben traded a high five. It was the last week of July. To most it meant the middle of summer. But for those living on Chincoteague Island, it meant the world-famous pony swim.

Willa couldn't wait to watch the wild ponies of Assateague Island swim across the channel to Chincoteague. Those who wanted an Assateague pony of their own could bid for one at the famous pony auction the next day.

"Do you think she remembers?" Willa asked as she patted the white star-shaped mark on Starbuck's butterscotch forehead.

"Remembers what?" Ben asked.

"Do you think Starbuck remembers swimming with the other ponies from Assateague to Chincoteague?" Willa asked.

"You know what they say," Ben said with a shrug. "A horse never forgets."

"I think that's an elephant." Willa smiled.

She couldn't wait for the pony swim in just two days. For the past ninety years, the world-famous event had taken place each summer. For Willa and Ben it would be their first.

Willa felt lucky to live on Chincoteague. A year ago the Dunlaps had moved from Chicago to the island where her mom grew up. Willa missed the city, but she loved the big old house her parents turned into an inn, her new friends, and most of all—having her own pony.

"I almost forgot something," Willa said, clutching Starbuck's rein to turn her around. "We promised Mom and Dad we'd help them today. Misty Inn is about to have a ton of visitors for the pony swim."

"Okay," Ben said as he slipped his foot into a stirrup, "but this time it's my turn to ride Starbuck."

Ben settled into the saddle. Willa took one last glance across the frothy white waters at Assateague Island. Then she, Ben, and Starbuck were on their way.

Willa walked her pony up the beach, then along the familiar trails leading to Misty Inn.

Starbuck seemed to know the way too, and she picked up her pace closer to home.

When they reached Misty Inn, their frisky puppy, Amos, was waiting outside the barn door. Amos loved the barn and the horses more than anything.

"I'll fill the water bucket," Ben said as Willa led Starbuck to her stall. Willa caught the horse gazing into the next stall, where their guest pony, Buttercup, stayed. But this week Buttercup's stall would be empty.

"I know you miss Buttercup, Starbuck," Willa said. "But she has an important job this week—to help Mr. Starling in the pony roundup."

Amos playfully jumped up at Ben as he carried a bucket of fresh water to Starbuck.

"You do remember the pony roundup," he asked. "Don't you, Starbuck?"

Starbuck gave a little snort.

Willa was about to grab Starbuck's currycomb when she heard her dad's voice calling from outside. "Willa, Ben, Grandma Edna's here!"

Willa and Ben exchanged surprised looks. It was the day of the pony vet check on Assateague Island. Grandma Edna was a vet, so what was she doing at Misty Inn?

"Hi, Grandma Edna!" Willa called as she and Ben raced over from the barn.

"Hi, yourselves!" Grandma Edna said. She stood next to Mom and Dad, her pickup truck nearby. A shopping bag hung from one hand as she petted a purring New Cat with her other.

Grandma Edna placed the bag on the ground to wrap her arms around Willa and Ben. She smelled like salt water and ponies, which told Willa one thing. . . .

"You were at the vet check today, Grandma Edna," Willa guessed excitedly. "Are the ponies ready for the big swim?"

"Resting up and ready as they'll ever be," Grandma Edna said. "But right now I come to Misty Inn with gifts and news."

"Grandma is being mysterious, kids," Mom added with a grin.

"What's in the bag, Grandma Edna?" Willa asked. "Something for Starbuck?"

"Or us?" Ben asked eagerly.

"Hold your horses, you two," Grandma Edna joked, and then continued. "It's just something I heard through the grapevine. Word has it some big-city travel critic will be staying at Misty Inn this week."

"Travel critic?" Dad repeated.

"Does he or she want to write about Misty Inn?" Mom asked.

Grandma Edna nodded. "For some travel magazine, I heard. So you'd all better be at the top of your game."

Willa's eyes widened at the news. She had heard of movie critics, who wrote about blockbuster films, but never travel critics.

"Misty Inn has been open for months," Mom told her own mother. "So we're always at the top of our game."

"Except the day the bathtub overflowed," Ben said. He smiled guiltily.

"Edna, if we weren't doing a good job," Dad added, "the inn wouldn't be booked solid with guests this week."

"One of those guests will be the travel critic," Grandma Edna said. She flapped her hand impatiently. "Oh, do what you want, but don't say I didn't warn you."

"Who is the critic, Grandma?" Willa asked as she picked up New Cat and held him close. "What's his or her name?"

"Wish I knew, honey," Grandma Edna said. "Most mystery critics go by some made-up name. So nobody at the inn will know who he or she is."

"Mystery critic?" Willa repeated as New Cat jumped out of her arms and scampered away. "You mean like a spy?"

Ben exclaimed, "Maybe he'll have awesome gadgets and land in our pasture in a black helicopter!"

"Ben, there will be no spies staying at Misty Inn this week," Mom insisted. "And if one of our guests happens to be a critic, we have nothing to worry about."

"We'll just do what we always do, kids," Dad added with a wink. "I'll cook mouthwatering meals for our restaurant, Family Farm, and your mom will run the inn like a tight ship as always."

"With your help," Mom said, raising an eyebrow at Willa and Ben. "Right?"

"Riiiiight," Willa and Ben said together.

But deep inside Willa was a bit worried. What if this mystery critic found something terribly wrong about Misty Inn and wrote a bad review? Would Mom and Dad have to close the inn? Would they have to move back to Chicago?

Apartment buildings don't allow horses, Willa thought. *What would we do with Starbuck?*

Grandma Edna interrupted Willa's worries. "Now for the gifts. They're just a few things to ensure a five-star rating from that mystery critic."

Grandma Edna carefully pulled out items from her bag that Willa recognized from Miller Farm—a colorful tablecloth and two throw pillows, all embroidered with horse scenes.

"Just a few vintage things for the inn," Grandma Edna explained. "You can display them to highlight the importance of the pony swim and auction this week."

"Or impress the critic?" Dad asked playfully. "Thanks, Edna. They're very nice."

"They are nice," Mom agreed. "But they're old, too. You've had them at Miller Farm since I was a little girl."

"I think they're neat," Willa said, reaching out to take the tablecloth and pillows from Grandma Edna. "The brown horse on the bigger pillow reminds me of Starbuck."

"Now there's a girl with good taste," Grandma Edna declared. "Amelia, Eric, I believe your daughter takes after me," she said, getting into her truck and driving off.

Willa considered that a huge compliment. To many, Grandma Edna was the best vet on Chincoteague Island. And Willa was thinking of becoming a vet when she grew up.

With Ben behind her, Willa carried the treasured heirlooms into the house.

"Willa, did you hear what Grandma Edna said?" Ben asked. "There's going to be a spy at Misty Inn."

"Not a spy, a travel critic," Willa corrected. She turned to Mom's office computer, where the week's guest list was open. "And it's superimportant, so we have to find out who he or she is so we can make sure this guest has an awesome time," Willa said.

"But how do we know who the travel critic is when he or she has a fake name?" Ben asked.

"We'll take a wild guess," Willa said.

She and Ben studied the list. Most guests were checking in tomorrow, the day before the pony swim. Only one guest, an Anthony Fox, was checking in today, Monday.

"Fox," Ben stated as he pointed to the screen. "That's got to be him, Willa. I know it."

"How?" Willa asked.

"Because he's using the name Fox," Ben explained, "and a mystery critic has got to be as sly—"

"As a fox," Willa finished. "Good work, Sherlock. Something tells me we found our mystery critic."

Chapter 2

"REMIND ME WHY WE'RE MUCKING THE BARN,"
Ben said, "when we just cleaned it this morning? And why we had to change our clothes?"

Ben grunted as he swung a broom to dust
cobwebs from underneath the loft.

"I told you," Willa said, sifting through
Starbuck's bedding with a pitchfork. "Mr. Fox
is checking in later."

"But he's sleeping in the inn," Ben said, "not in the barn."

"Mr. Fox might peek inside the barn to see how clean it is," Willa explained. "Let's hope he doesn't peek inside your room."

Willa stopped raking to glance out the barn door to the pasture. Amos was running circles around Starbuck as she grazed calmly.

"What do we do when Mr. Fox gets here?" Ben asked.

Willa quickly pulled a piece of paper from her pants pocket. "This morning, after we finished grooming Starbuck, I went upstairs and made a list."

Willa was *always* making lists to organize her thoughts. And her family loved teasing her about them. This one was called Operation Mr. Fox:

1. Greet Mr. Fox by name.
2. Carry his bags to his room.
3. Make sure he has everything
   he needs.

"'Everything he needs'?" Ben asked, reading over Willa's shoulder. "What if he loves hot-fudge sundaes and wants a hot-fudge fountain right in the middle of his room?"

Willa rolled her eyes. "Ben, be serious."

As she folded her list and slipped it inside her pocket, she heard the familiar crunchy sound of a car on the gravelly driveway.

Peeking outside the barn, Willa and Ben saw a dark-haired man stepping out of his car.

"Hello," Mom greeted him, walking over from the inn. "Are you checking in today?"

"Sure am," the man called back. "I'm Anthony Fox."

Fox? Willa turned to Ben and whispered, "It's him."

"But he wasn't supposed to get here until later," Ben hissed. "What do we do?"

"The first thing on the list," Willa whispered. "Meet and greet."

"But our clothes are covered with mud and sawdust," Ben called after Willa as she hurried out of the barn. "And maybe worse stuff."

By the time Willa and Ben reached the car, Mom was busily talking to Mr. Fox. But they stopped when Willa called out, "Good afternoon, Mr. Fox. We hope you had a pleasant drive to Misty Inn."

"Welcome to Chincoteague Island!" Ben

boomed with a wave of his hand. "Home of the world-famous pony swim."

"Um . . . thank you," Mr. Fox blurted.

Mom curiously studied Willa and Ben, and then she said, "I was just about to help Mr. Fox with his bags."

"We'll do it," Willa and Ben said in unison.

"Thanks, but I only have one duffel bag," Mr. Fox said, pulling a medium-size bag from the front seat of his car. "I can easily carry it myself."

Mr. Fox's phone suddenly rang. When he answered, Mom whispered to Willa and Ben.

"Kids, Mr. Fox just told me he's allergic to cats and dogs, so I'm putting New Cat outside. Make sure Amos doesn't come into the house either, okay?"

Willa nodded. Her friend Kate from Chicago was allergic to pets, and it wasn't fun. "Okay, Mom," she said, but his allergies did concern her a bit.

Mom shot Willa and Ben one more confused look before walking back to the house.

Mr. Fox was still on the phone, his duffel bag at his feet.

"I got it," Willa said, snatching it up.

"No, let me," Ben argued.

Mr. Fox ended his call just as Willa and Ben had begun a tug-of-war with his bag.

"Um . . . it's got two handles," Mr. Fox suggested. "Why don't you both carry it?"

Willa grabbed one handle, Ben the other, and Mr. Fox followed as they carried it up the stairs to his room.

To Willa, Mr. Fox seemed young, more like a college student than a professional travel critic, unless . . . that was his disguise!

"You'll be staying in the Blue Room," Willa called over her shoulder halfway up the stairs. "You may notice the vintage horse pillows on the bed as well as the horse-themed tablecloth on the dresser."

"You mean Grandma Edna's?" Ben whispered to Willa. "When did you put those in there?"

"After I wrote my list," Willa whispered back. "It was on my other list of things to do in the Blue Room."

Once on the second floor, Willa used her free hand to open the door to the Blue Room. With a shy thank you, Mr. Fox stepped inside.

"Four-poster bed, antique furniture," he observed. "Nice."

"The flowers on the dresser are fresh," Willa pointed out. "And the window has the most awesome view of the ocean."

"You can watch the whole pony swim on

Wednesday from the comfort of your room," Ben added.

Mr. Fox started to answer, but instead of words, out came a loud, *"Ah-chooo!"*

As Mr. Fox sniffed and searched his pockets for a tissue, Willa turned frantically to Ben. "I forgot to put a tissue box in the room," she whispered. "Go get one from Mom."

"Be right back," Ben promised. He waved through the door at Mr. Fox and said, "Spy—I mean bye!"

Still sniffing, Mr. Fox turned to Willa and said, "I'll take my bag now."

Willa handed the duffel bag to Mr. Fox, but not before dusting sawdust specks from the handle.

"Thanks for your help," Mr. Fox said. He gave Willa one last smile before shutting the door.

So far so good, Willa thought to herself. She was about to go downstairs when another sneeze stopped her in her tracks.

Willa froze as several more sneezes exploded from behind the door. She was sure New Cat wasn't under the bed and Amos was hanging out at the barn—so what was up?

"Ben!" Willa shouted down the stairs. "We need to get those tissues. Quick!"

Chapter 3

"REMEMBER, BEN," WILLA TOLD HER BROTHER the next morning. "We should recommend the seafood omelet to Mr. Fox, with fresh fruit salad and rolls on the side."

Ben stood next to Willa in the kitchen. Both peeked into the Family Farm dining room as the guests ate breakfast. There was nothing suspicious about the other guests. So far Mr. Fox was their number one mystery critic suspect!

"What if he just wants scrambled eggs?" Ben asked.

"Then we ask if he'd like Dad's scrambled eggs with mushrooms and chives," Willa said. "Dad's cooking is one of the best parts of Misty Inn, so we have to make sure Mr. Fox tries it."

"And writes an awesome review," Ben added with a nod. "Got it."

Willa's eyes searched the tables for Mr. Fox. Almost every table was filled with breakfast-eating guests most likely chatting about the pony swim tomorrow.

Willa was excited about the pony swim too. But right now all she could think about was the mysterious Mr. Fox. *Where could he be?*

"Why isn't Mr. Fox having breakfast?" Willa asked.

"Maybe he overslept," Ben suggested, "which would be a very good sign."

"A good sign? Why?" Willa asked.

"It would mean his bed was nice and comfy," Ben explained.

Willa thought Ben might have a point, but just then someone darted past them through the kitchen. Mr. Fox?! He had a crumpled tissue in one hand, his duffel bag in the other. Where was he going in such a hurry?

"I'm so sorry, Mr. Fox," Mom called after him. "I didn't know you had such an uncomfortable night."

Willa stared at Ben. "Uncomfortable night"? What did that mean?

By the time Willa and Ben stepped outside, they were too late. Mr. Fox's car was zooming away from Misty Inn.

Starbuck stood in the pasture, her ears pointed in the direction of the car. It seemed even she knew something was wrong.

"I don't get it," Mom said. "New Cat wasn't

in Mr. Fox's room. Neither was Amos. Yet he said he was up all night long sneezing."

"What do you think it was?" Ben asked.

"Someone put your grandma's old horse pillows and tablecloth in his room," Mom explained. "I'll bet it was your dad. He said he didn't want them in the living room."

Willa didn't have to look at Ben to know he was staring at her. They both knew it was Willa, not Dad, who was guilty. She had put the vintage pillow and tablecloth in Mr. Fox's room, not Dad!

Mom continued explaining, "Since Grandma Edna had them at Miller Farm, I'll bet they're probably coated with animal hair, dander, and feathers. Not a great match for Mr. Fox's allergies."

"Oh, Mom. Why would he ever have come to a farm?" Willa blurted. She was about to confess when Ben heaved a big sigh. . . .

"There goes our awesome review," Ben said.

"Review? What do you mean?" Mom asked.

"Mr. Fox was the mystery travel critic, right?" Ben asked. "Because he's as sly as a fox."

Mom stared at Ben. "Mr. Fox is a graphic artist, not a critic. He heard how nice Chincoteague Island was and wanted to propose to his girlfriend here."

"Propose?" Ben said, wrinkling his nose. "As in getting married?"

Mom nodded. "He came to Chincoteague for one day to see if the setting was right. But after his animal allergies kicked in, he decided to propose in the city."

Willa was relieved but also disappointed. If Mr. Fox wasn't the critic, who was?

"Willa, Ben," Mom said gently, "even if one of our guests is a travel critic, we shouldn't be doing anything different this week."

She then flashed a smile and said, "I have an idea. Why don't you both take a break from your chores and go over to the Starlings' for a while."

Willa smiled too. "I like that idea, Mom."

"Me too," Ben agreed.

Sarah and Chipper Starling were Willa's and Ben's best friends since moving to Chincoteague Island. Willa knew the Starling kids would be super-excited about the pony swim tomorrow. Their dad was a saltwater cowboy, one of the riders herding the swimming ponies from

Assateague to Chincoteague. And this year Mr. Starling would be riding Buttercup.

"Maybe Sarah and Chipper will let us use their zip line in the backyard," Willa told Ben.

"Sure, they'll let us," Ben said, pointing at his chest with his thumb. "I did help build the Zipster, you know."

"Just be sure to get home before dinner," Mom called over her shoulder on the way to the house. "With the pony swim tomorrow, the dining room will be full with guests."

And one of those guests, Willa thought, *might be the mystery travel critic.*

Chapter 4

"AVAST, YE SCURVY DOG!" BEN SHOUTED AS HE rode the Zipster from the tree house down to the lawn. "Prepare to surrender yer ship!"

Chipper waved a bright blue glow stick from the other side of the zip line. "Not without a fight," he growled. "You kraken-breathed blaggard!"

Sarah rolled her eyes as she sat on the grass

next to Willa. "It's not even Talk Like a Pirate Day." She sighed.

Willa was hardly paying attention to their brothers. She was too busy thinking about the Misty Inn mystery man—or woman.

"Sarah, do you think the critic is a he or a she?" Willa asked. She had already filled in her best friend about what had happened.

"It doesn't make a difference," Sarah said. "The most important thing is finding out who he or she is."

"Even though Mom told us not to?" Willa asked.

Sarah nodded and said, "Your mom probably doesn't know it, but a bad review can make or break a business in a small town like this."

"How do *you* know?" Willa asked.

"My mother's friend Delores owned a café on Chincoteague a few years ago," Sarah explained. "It was really, really popular until a customer found a horsefly in her macaroni and cheese."

Willa wrinkled her nose. "Ewww."

"Even worse—the woman turned out to be a mystery food critic," Sarah explained, "who wrote all about Delores's mac and fleas!"

"Great," Willa groaned.

"Did someone say mystery?" somebody asked.

Willa turned to see her other friend Lena. The only thing Lena loved more than mystery books and TV shows was solving mysteries herself.

"A mystery travel critic might be staying

at the inn this week," Willa explained. "Ben and I want to make sure Misty Inn gets a good review. It's really important."

"Not just a *good* review, Willa," Ben chimed in as he and Chipper raced over. "*Awesome.*"

Willa told Lena everything about Mr. Fox. "We thought we'd found our mystery critic," Willa said, "but now we're back to square one."

"Well, it's a good thing I'm here to help," Lena said, sitting on the grass next to the others. "What do you know so far about the person who's coming?"

"Not much," Willa admitted. She reached into her pocket and pulled out a piece of note-paper from Mom's desk. "It could be any of these guests staying at Misty Inn for the pony swim."

Lena scrunched her brow as she studied the list of guests who would check into Misty Inn that day.

Blue Room: Mr. Frank Ross of Virginia, traveling alone.

Red Room: Mrs. Andrea Iori and her daughter, Yuki, from Philadelphia.

Green Room: Mrs. Ida and Mr. Elmer Green from Ohio.

After a few seconds Lena announced, "Done. I found your mystery travel critic."

"How did you do that?" Ben asked.

"Through the process of elimination," Lena said, pronouncing each word carefully. "The first suspect out is Mr. Ross. I don't think he's your guy."

"But he's a man traveling alone," Willa pointed out. "So he could be working."

"You had a man traveling alone at the inn last night," Lena reminded. "How did that work out for you?"

"Not good." Willa sighed.

Next Lena pointed to Ida and Elmer Green on the list. "They're out too," she said.

"Why?" Willa asked.

"Because Ida and Elmer are old-fashioned

names," Lena pointed out. "They're probably retired and here for the pony swim, not to write a review."

"That leaves Mrs. Iori and her daughter, Yuki," Sarah said. "Why would a mystery writer bring her daughter along on a job?"

"Because Yuki would be the perfect distraction while she scopes the place," Lena explained. "Spies in the movies use distractions all the time."

Willa stared at Lena. Her friend's over-the-top imagination was making her head spin. So was trying to figure out who the mystery travel critic was. And with such a busy week ahead, that was the last thing Willa really needed, so . . .

"Maybe Mom was right," Willa said, folding

the list. "Maybe we shouldn't waste time try-ing to find a person who may not even show up. Maybe these aren't even their real names!"

"Waste time?" Sarah repeated. "But I told you what happened to my mom's friend Delores."

"That will never happen at Misty Inn, Sarah," Willa said, shaking her head. "Or at Family Farm restaurant."

"Why not?" Sarah asked.

"Because mac and fleas is not on the menu," Willa joked.

After taking one last ride on the Zipster and paying Buttercup a visit, it was time to head home.

"Remember, you guys!" Chipper called to Willa and Ben. "You're watching the pony swim from our skiff tomorrow."

"Arrgh!" Ben shouted back to Chipper pirate-style. "Yer'll be watching from the crow's nest, ye scalawag!"

"Ben." Willa sighed. "Seriously?"

Once home, Ben ran inside for a snack. But Willa wanted to check on Starbuck.

Starbuck nickered happily when she saw Willa. The moment Willa opened the stall door, the pony nudged the pocket of her shorts— her way of saying she wanted a snack too.

Willa never left the house without a treat or two for Starbuck or other ponies.

"Bon appétit," Willa declared, and then she giggled as Starbuck nibbled a string bean from her flat palm. No matter how often she fed her pony, it always tickled.

"Tomorrow's the big day, girl," Willa said as she stroked Starbuck's velvety forehead. "Maybe you'll see some old friends from Assateague Island."

Starbuck inhaled, then puffed breath out her nostrils. Willa knew Starbuck wouldn't watch the big swim tomorrow, but she loved thinking her pony was just as excited as she was.

After getting Starbuck fresh water, Willa gave her pony's ear a final scratch. "Time to help Mom and Dad now," she said.

Willa left the barn, closing the door behind her. As she turned she noticed a shiny red car pulling up behind the inn. The car stopped, and the door on the driver's side opened. Willa watched as a woman stepped out. She wore slim black pants, a white sleeveless blouse, and sleek sunglasses.

Slung over one bare shoulder was a large canvas bag.

After a few seconds the passenger door opened and a girl stepped out. She was dressed more sportily in cargo shorts, a gray T-shirt, and a red baseball cap.

Willa tried to figure out the girl's age. She looked about nine. Or maybe nine and a half. Maybe even ten.

Most of our guests are older, Willa thought. *It'll be great to have someone close to my age at the inn. I wonder if she's nice—*

The girl might have felt someone watching her, because she turned and looked straight at Willa. Willa felt her cheeks burn—embarrassed to be caught staring. But the girl smiled. It was a shy smile but a friendly one.

Willa gave a little wave and called, "Hi."

The girl waved back just as Ben charged out of the house to help with their luggage. The woman seemed happy to have Ben lug their bags—just not her canvas one.

As the three filed into the house, Willa had a pretty good idea who the guests were. The woman was probably Mrs. Iori. The girl could be her daughter, Yuki.

But were they actually the restaurant reviewers, with Yuki as the distraction, as Lena suggested?

Chapter 5

WILLA BRUSHED HER HAIR UNTIL IT WAS NICE and shiny. Next she stood in front of her full-length mirror making sure her sundress was crisp, her sandals mud-free. After a day of stall mucking and zip lining, she was finally clean and ready for dinner.

Thoughts of the mystery travel critic were

no longer on Willa's mind. She was too excited about the pony swim the next day. And about having a guest her age at the inn.

"Ben, guess what?" Willa asked once out in the hallway. Ben was also cleanly dressed with his hair actually combed. "I saw the girl who's—"

"Me first," Ben pleaded. "You're not going to believe this. Not in a million years."

"Believe what?" Willa asked.

Ben leaned forward, whispering, "One of the guests who just checked in has got to be the mystery travel critic."

Willa's shoulders dropped. Not again.

"Ben," Willa complained, "from now on I want to concentrate on the pony swim."

"But while you were getting ready, that man traveling alone, Mr. Ross, checked in," Ben said. "When I went to help him with his bag, he wouldn't let me touch it!"

"So?" Willa said. "Lots of guests want to carry their own bags."

"This was a plain black briefcase," Ben said, his eyes wide. "When I grabbed the handle, he grabbed it too. Then he stared me straight in the eye and refused to let go."

"Maybe he has important papers in his brief-case," Willa guessed.

"Sure," Ben said, narrowing his eyes. "Important travel critic papers!"

Willa had to admit—this new guest did sound mysterious. Mysterious enough to make them wonder about the mystery travel critic all over again.

"That was my news," Ben said. "What's yours?"

Somehow, talking to Ben about Yuki didn't seem so urgent anymore. "I'll show you later in the dining room, Ben. But remember, we don't know for sure if Mr. Ross is the travel critic."

"It could be any of the guests," Ben said as they headed down the stairs to the kitchen. "So let's treat them all like kings and queens."

Willa refused to go that far. But she did want all their guests to love Misty Inn as much as she did. And a big part of what she loved about Misty Inn was her dad's cooking.

"Dad, these fish sticks are delicious," Willa said as she and Ben finished their dinners in the kitchen.

Dad was hunched over a chopping board on the big butcher-block table. He was slicing mushrooms so fast his hands seemed a blur.

"That's actually panko-crusted fish sticks with an herb dipping sauce," Dad explained. "I thought the girl who checked in with her mom might like them."

"You mean Yuki," Willa said, swirling her fish stick in the sauce. "I saw her and her mom check in before. She looks very nice."

"Distractions usually are," Ben said.

"Distractions?" Mom asked as she walked into the kitchen. "What distractions?"

"It's nothing, Mom," Willa answered, and turned to her father to quickly change the subject. "Dad," she asked, "did you ever cook this at the fancy hotel you used to work at in Chicago?"

"Sometimes," Dad said.

"What was so fancy about that hotel?" Ben asked.

"Well, at check-in each guest was greeted at the desk with a glass of fresh orange juice and a hot towel," Dad explained. "And every night they would find an expensive chocolate on their pillows."

"So they would have sweet dreams!" Willa joked.

Ben's eyes flashed. He jumped up, placed his empty plate in the sink, then dashed out of the kitchen.

"Where's he off to?" Mom asked. "You both know you have a very special job tonight in the dining room, right?"

Willa nodded. "To tell the guests what's on the dessert menu."

"And that means carrying this," Dad said as he pulled a platter out of the refrigerator.

Willa's mouth watered at the sight of the dessert platter. It overflowed with the most yummy-looking desserts her dad had ever baked.

Willa lifted the platter to make sure she could hold it. She then described each dessert one by one—exactly as she would do for the guests.

"Good evening," Willa practiced. "Our desserts tonight are lemon chiffon cake with strawberry cream frosting, chocolate fudge brownie with whipped cream, assorted cookies, and an all-natural raspberry sorbet."

"Which will be a puddle if you don't hurry," Mom said with a smile.

Ben came back into the kitchen, grabbed a pad from the counter, and said, "I'll write down the orders."

With Ben at her side, Willa carefully carried the desserts into the dining room.

"There's Mr. Ross talking on his phone," Ben said, nodding toward a table against the wall. "Hopefully he's reporting on the most awesome meal of his life."

Willa was more interested in the diners near the window. That's where Yuki and her mom sat. Mrs. Iori had changed into another trendy summer outfit. Yuki was still dressed in her cargo shorts but now with a red T-shirt.

"Let's start with the nearest table, where that older couple is," Ben suggested. "Then we can work our way back."

As Willa brought over the dessert platter, the guest's voice excitedly boomed. "Well, now, Ida, as if that scrumptious seafood casserole wasn't enough, look what we have here."

The woman smiled back. "This must be our lucky day, Elmer."

Willa grinned. Just as she guessed, it was Ida and Elmer Green—the retired couple who probably were *not* the mystery critics.

"I know exactly what I want," Elmer said cheerily. "That raspberry sorbet looks nifty. I'll have that."

Ida tapped her chin thoughtfully as she eyed the desserts. "That brownie. Is it milk chocolate or dark chocolate? And is that topping butter-cream or whipped?"

Willa wasn't too sure but said, "Our dad likes to use dark chocolate and whipped cream, but we can check—"

"Not necessary, dear," Ida interrupted. "Now, if I wanted a different flavor of sorbet, would I be able to get it?"

Willa nodded. "Besides raspberry, we have lemon and coconut."

"Splendid," Ida said. "In that case I'll have the assorted cookies."

Willa and Ben traded surprised looks. After all those questions about the brownie and sorbet, Ida ordered cookies? Was that suspicious?

Whatever.

Ben wrote down Ida's order. As they headed to the next table, he whispered, "Now let's see what James Bond wants for dessert."

Mr. Ross was still busy on the phone, his briefcase under the table. He stopped speaking when he saw Willa and Ben.

"What have we here?" Mr. Ross asked, smiling at the desserts.

Willa described the desserts one by one. When she was done, Mr. Ross ordered the chiffon cake and a cup of coffee.

"Excellent choice, sir," Ben declared, writing on his pad with a flourish. As they turned away from the table, Mr. Ross went back to his call, speaking loudly enough for Willa and Ben to hear. . . .

"You know I'm on a secret mission," Mr. Ross said. "I'll do the best I can."

Secret mission?

Ben shook Willa's arm, almost making her drop the desserts. "Willa, did you hear that?" he hissed. "He said he's on a secret mission."

"I heard," Willa said. Ben was right. Mr. Ross sounded more mysterious by the minute.

Willa and Ben served more desserts, saving the Ioris' table for last.

"Hi," Willa greeted Mrs. Iori and Yuki. "I'm Willa Dunlap, and this is my brother, Ben."

"We're the Ioris," the woman said with a warm smile. "I'm Andrea, and this is Yuki. She's ten."

"I saw you standing by the barn before," Yuki said to Willa, her voice excited. "Are there any animals in it?"

Willa nodded and said, "My pony, Starbuck. Maybe you can both meet her while you're here."

"That's a nice offer, Willa, but I'll pass," Mrs. Iori said. "Seeing all the swimming ponies tomorrow will be plenty for me."

Mrs. Iori continued, "I came to Chincoteague Island to work."

"'Work'?" Ben repeated. Willa caught him raising an eyebrow. "What kind of work?"

Before Mrs. Iori could answer, Yuki smiled at Willa and chimed in, "I'd like to watch the pony swim. I can never see too many ponies."

That gave Willa an idea.

"Ben and I are watching the pony swim from our friends' skiff tomorrow," Willa told the Ioris. "I can find out if there's room for both of you."

"What's a skiff?" Yuki asked.

"It's a small boat with a motor," Ben explained. "We'll be so close to the swimming ponies we'll be able to feed them carrots!"

"Really?" Yuki gasped.

"No, not really." Willa giggled. "But we will

be closer than if we watched them from the beach."

"Can we, Mom?" Yuki asked. "Please?"

Mrs. Iori thoughtfully looked from Willa to Ben to Yuki. "I'm not sure," she answered slowly. "Will there be an adult in the boat?"

"Mrs. Starling will drive it," Willa explained. "She and Mr. Starling give boat tours off the island, so she's an expert."

"We'll all wear life jackets, too," Ben said. "And lots of bug spray for the mosquitoes."

"Lovely," Mrs. Iori mumbled sarcastically.

"May I go, Mom?" Yuki asked again.

"Well . . . I could stay here and work on my photographs," Mrs. Iori thought out loud. "Let me think about it."

Photographs? Willa remembered the big

case Mrs. Iori had slung over her shoulder. Was it a camera case?

Ben wasted no time asking his next question: "What kind of photographs do you take, Mrs. Iori?"

Before Mrs. Iori could answer, Yuki chimed in again.

"I hope I can go to the pony swim," Yuki said. "Seeing the ponies up close would be so sweet."

Sweet! Willa suddenly remembered her platter of desserts. The raspberry sorbet was melting like a warm snowball.

"We have an assortment of desserts," Willa spoke super-quickly. "May we recommend the lemon chiffon cake with strawberry cream?"

"Yuki doesn't like strawberries," Mrs. Iori said. "But she loves blueberries."

"Mo-om!" Yuki groaned, embarrassed to have her mother speak for her.

"No problem," Ben piped up.

Willa shot her brother a sideways glance. Dad hadn't made blueberry topping for dinner. What was Ben thinking?

"I'll just have a cup of coffee with milk on the side please," Mrs. Iori said with a small nod. "Thanks, kids."

As they walked away from the Ioris' table, Willa whispered, "Dad only has strawberry topping today."

"So he'll whip up blueberry, too," Ben whispered back. "Mrs. Iori could be taking secret photographs of Misty Inn. She could be the mystery travel critic, too. We have to make them happy."

One person who wasn't happy about the blueberries was Dad.

"How could you tell our guest I have blueberry cream when I don't?" Dad asked in the kitchen.

"I promised Yuki, Dad," Ben admitted. "You and Mom always say a promise is a promise, right?"

"Right," Dad groaned, pulling open the fridge. "We still have whipped cream and leftover blueberry compote from breakfast. But no fresh blueberries for the garnish."

He turned to Willa and Ben and said, "Unless . . . you two go outside and quickly pick a few."

"*Now?*" Willa asked.

"But it's going to be dark soon," Ben said.

"Not for another two hours," Dad said. His eyes twinkled as he added, "And a promise is a promise. Right?"

"Riiight," Willa and Ben chorused.

Willa and Ben soon found themselves outside picking blueberries for Yuki's dessert. The hot summer sun had faded to a hazy yellow spot in the sky. In the distance Starbuck stood in the pasture, her shaggy brown tail flicking mosquitoes.

"Remember when we first moved here and I was so quiet?" Ben asked when their bucket had enough blueberries.

"Yeah." Willa chuckled. "What a difference a year makes."

They were about to head back inside when Mom rushed outside. Stretched between both hands was a white pillowcase. Stuck to the pillowcase was an icky-looking half-melted chocolate bar!

"Mr. Ross went up to his room and found this," Mom said. She raised an eyebrow. "Any idea how a chocolate bar got on his pillow?"

"Um . . . sort of," Ben admitted. "Dad said fancy hotels leave chocolates on the pillows." He shrugged his shoulders and said, "But I didn't think my chocolate bar would melt."

Mom stared at Ben. Willa stared at the pillowcase. Then suddenly—"Neeeeiiiiiighhhh!"

All three heads turned toward the pasture. Willa knew a pony laugh when she heard it, which made her laugh too. Then Ben. Then Mom.

The goopy chocolate bar on the pillowcase wasn't really funny, but after a long, tiring day, everyone needed a good laugh. Including Starbuck!

Chapter 6

"WILLA... TIME TO GET UP."

Willa's eyes stayed shut as she heard the faint sound of her mother's voice. Was it part of her dream?

"The pony swim is today, Willa," Mom said.

Pony swim? Willa heard that loud and clear. She smiled as her eyes snapped open. Who needed sleep when her real dream was about to come true?

Willa rolled out of bed. The bedside lamp had been turned on. It was so early in the morning that the sky outside her window was still black.

In a flash Willa was washed and dressed. She practically ran down the stairs to the kitchen, where preparations for the pony swim were underway. Dad and Katherine Starling, Sarah's teenage sister, were busy filling express breakfast bags for guests. Katherine worked part-time at Misty Inn and was a huge help.

Ben yawned as he scribbled the words "Pony Express" on each bag with a blue marker. "Why did we have to get up so early?" he asked. "The ponies aren't swimming for another few hours."

"Katherine already told us," Dad said as he placed a freshly baked scone into a bag. "The pony swim can cause a traffic jam of boats on the channel."

Katherine nodded. "My mom wants to leave early and get a good spot before she anchors."

Willa pointed to the Pony Express bags Ben was stuffing and said, "I hope there are no soggy chocolate bars in there."

"Very funny," Ben said with a smirk.

Willa turned to Katherine. "Will you be coming with us on the boat?" she asked.

"Not this year," Katherine answered. "I'm watching the swim from the beach with my friends."

Willa listed the passengers who would be in

Mrs. Starling's boat. "Lena won't be there—she's watching the swim and parade with her family, so there'll be Mrs. Starling, me, Ben, Sarah, Chipper—"

"And me!" someone cut in.

Turning, Willa saw Yuki at the kitchen door. She was wearing shorts, a T-shirt, a white cap, and a smile.

"Good morning, Yuki," Dad greeted.

"It's an awesome morning," Yuki declared. "My mom said I could watch the pony swim from the boat today."

"Cool!" Willa said.

"That is good news, Yuki," Mom said, walking into the kitchen. She stopped at the counter to fill her coffee cup. "Is your mom going too?"

"No, Mrs. Dunlap," Yuki said. "Mom's checking her camera for the pictures she wants to take today."

Ben looked up from the bag he was stuffing. "Pictures?" he asked. "What kind of pictures?"

"I'm not sure," Yuki replied. "I just know they're for some magazine."

Before Ben could ask which magazine, Yuki turned to Willa, her eyes shining. "Did you feed your pony yet?" she asked.

"I was just going to," Willa replied. "Would you like to watch?"

"Absolutely," Yuki said. "Just let me tell my mom I'm going to the barn."

As Yuki raced upstairs, Dad said, "Looks like you have a new friend, Willa."

"Her mother's very nice too," Mom said.

"Yeah," Ben whispered to Willa. "For a spy!"

The hot July sun was beginning to rise as Willa and Yuki made their way to the barn.

Once they stepped inside, Yuki took a long, deep breath. "Mmm," she said with a smile. "It's exactly how I thought a barn would smell."

Willa stared at Yuki. "Most guests hold their noses when they come in here," she said. "You really do love horses, don't you?"

Yuki saw Starbuck and gave a little gasp. She walked ahead of Willa straight to her stall.

"Yuki, meet Starbuck," Willa introduced. "Starbuck, meet Yuki Iori."

The gentle mare nuzzled Yuki's shoulder to say hello. "You are so lucky to have your own pony, Willa," Yuki said.

"Starbuck isn't just any pony," Willa said. "She's a real Assateague pony who swam to Chincoteague."

"No way," Yuki exclaimed.

"It's true," Willa told her. "Starbuck started out as a boarder at my grandma Edna's animal rescue center."

"Was she hurt?"

"Starbuck's leg was injured, but my grandma Edna is a vet and treated it," Willa explained. "She also let Ben and me groom and exercise Starbuck."

"So after a while she was able to walk?" Yuki asked.

"Not just that," Willa continued. "Starbuck walked all the way from Miller Farm to Misty Inn. That's when we knew she was finally home."

"That is so cool," Yuki said.

She then looked around the barn and asked, "Where do you keep the water and feed buckets? And Starbuck's brushes?"

Willa wasn't sure she wanted Yuki to groom Starbuck. She seemed to know a lot about ponies, but did she know about grooming them?

"How do you know so much about horses, Yuki?" Willa asked.

Yuki sighed. "I read everything I can about them."

Willa decided to start Yuki off with a simple task. She pointed to a rubber hose coiled up near the wall. A few inches away was a water bucket.

"Why don't you use that hose to fill the bucket with some fresh water?" she told Yuki.

"How much water?" Yuki asked.

"Almost to the top," Willa replied.

While Yuki filled the water bucket, Willa scooped feed into Starbuck's pail. "Maybe, if there's time, we can go riding together while you're here, Yuki," she said.

"I don't think so," Yuki said. "My mom doesn't like ponies much, so she never lets me ride."

Willa stopped scooping to look up. Not like ponies? How can anyone not like ponies? But Willa gave Yuki a reassuring smile and said, "You'll see more ponies today than you ever dreamed or read about."

"I can't wait!" Yuki said as she carried fresh water to Starbuck's stall.

Yuki turned out to be a quick learner. She fed Starbuck then helped groom her coat with three different types of brushes.

After the barn chores were done, Willa and Yuki returned to the house. Mrs. Iori was eating an early breakfast in the dining room, her camera case ready to go.

"Remember, Yuki," Mrs. Iori said. "Reapply sunscreen every hour on the boat. And please don't get near those ponies."

"I'll try, Mom." Yuki sighed. On the way out of the room, she whispered to Willa, "See what I mean? My mom isn't exactly a pony fan."

The sun was already high when Mrs. Starling dropped anchor in the channel. The skiff had a full crew. Willa, Yuki, and Ben shared a storage bench in the middle. Sarah and Chipper sat on cushioned seats. The skipper of the skiff, Mrs. Starling, sat before the outboard motor.

Willa breathed in the welcoming scent of warm salt water and coconut sunscreen. She still couldn't believe she was at an annual Chincoteague pony swim. She also couldn't believe how many skiffs, tour boats, and kayaks crammed the channel, all there for a glimpse of the world-famous swimming ponies.

"Check out the great view, kids," Mrs. Starling said, popping a straw sun hat over her brown hair. "It looks like we have the best seats in the house."

"Like getting tickets to the World Series with seats behind home plate," Chipper declared. "Way to go, Mom!"

Yuki gazed out at the thousands of people on the beach. Many were standing waist-deep in the water. A few had climbed trees for a better look.

"Look how many people are here," Yuki said excitedly. "It's like the ponies are celebrities."

"The ponies *are* celebrities, Yuki," Willa said, smiling.

"Yeah," Sarah agreed. "Who needs Hollywood when you can live in Chincoteague?"

The *Starling Sundancer* sloshed in the water as everyone waited for slack tide. That's when the ponies would begin their swim. During that time, Ben took every chance he could get to question Yuki about her mom.

"Um . . . Yuki, those pictures your mom is taking," Ben said, trying to act casual, "not that I really care . . . but what magazine are they for?"

"I don't know the name of it," Yuki said, pulling a muffin from her Pony Express bag. "Just that it's some travel magazine."

"Travel magazine," Ben whispered to Willa, "as in mystery travel critic!"

"Not now, Ben, please," Willa whispered back. "We're here to watch the pony swim."

The kids made the best of the wait, sharing stories, feeding hungry seagulls, even groaning at Chipper's corny pony riddles. . . .

"What's a vampire's favorite part of a horse race?" Chipper joked.

"When it's neck and neck." Sarah sighed. "You told us that one already, Chipper!"

Chipper was about to try another one when the crackling sound of a distant loudspeaker filled the air. A hush fell over the crowd before an announcer welcomed one and all to the pony swim.

Willa drew in an excited breath. Was this it? She soon got her answer when many began shouting, "Here they come! Here come the ponies!"

All eyes in the Starling skiff turned toward Assateague. The island was far but near enough for Willa to see what she had waited all year to see—a team of saltwater cowboys herding brown, black, and pinto ponies from the marshy sands into the water!

"Woo-hoo!" Ben cheered.

"Use the binoculars, kids," Mrs. Starling suggested. "You'll get a closer look."

There were plenty of binoculars to go around on the Starlings' tour boat. When Yuki looked through hers, she began to shout, "They're swimming. The ponies are swimming!"

Willa watched a parade of shaggy heads bobbing above the channel waters, moving toward Chincoteague. It was exactly the way she had dreamed it would be. Even better!

"Why are they all swimming in the same direction?" Yuki asked.

"Ponies are herd animals," Mrs. Starling explained. "They prefer to travel in groups."

But after a few seconds it seemed Mrs. Starling had spoken too soon. Because bobbing away from the herd and in the direction of their skiff was a wide-eyed buckskin foal.

"Oooh, look at her!" Yuki gasped. "She's perfect!"

"How do you know it's a she?" Sarah asked.

"I just do," Yuki insisted, then stretched her hand out toward the swimming foal.

Willa lowered her binoculars to watch the foal with her own eyes. The little pony seemed to be swimming straight toward Yuki's hand. But just as she got close enough for Willa to see her soft brown eyes—

SPLASH-SPLASH-SPLASH!

Willa looked past the foal. A saltwater

cowboy was steering his own pony toward the swim-away foal. The cowboy was Mr. Starling. His pony was Buttercup!

Mr. Starling skillfully rode Buttercup around the foal, turning her in the direction of the herd. After a bit of coaxing the little foal rejoined the herd swimming toward Chincoteague.

"Good job, Dad!" Sarah cheered.

"Way to go, Buttercup!" Chipper added.

Mr. Starling turned and tipped his cowboy hat with a grin. Then he and Buttercup splashed their way back to the herd.

When Willa turned to Yuki, she was still leaning forward, her hand stretched out.

"Yuki?" Mrs. Starling called. "No leaning out of the boat, please."

Yuki pulled her hand back in the boat, but her eyes were still on the herd. Willa had a pretty good idea she was looking for the little foal.

By now the swimming ponies were stepping out of the water onto Chincoteague's marshy shoreline. Willa put the binoculars to her eyes again, watching as the crowd spread out to make room for dozens of wet, shiny ponies. Many squealed happily as the ponies shook water out of their thick, soggy manes.

"Our first pony swim, Willa," Ben declared when all the ponies were ashore. "How cool was that?"

"Very," Willa agreed. She turned to Yuki. "What did you think, Yuki? What was your favorite part?"

"I'll bet it was seeing all those beautiful ponies," Mrs. Starling said with a wink.

Yuki shook her head. "No, Mrs. Starling. It was seeing *one* beautiful pony, the adorable little foal that swam toward our boat." Yuki looked toward the beach and smiled. "And I hope I see her again."

Willa smiled. Yuki's mom may not have been a pony fan, but Yuki made up for it—in a huge way.

Chapter 7

MRS. STARLING AND THE KIDS SCRAMBLED TO
get the boat docked. Willa helped Chipper cover
the skiff.

"I waited all year for the pony swim," Willa
said a bit sadly, "and now it's over."

Chipper smiled at Willa from the other side
of the boat. "The swim may be over, but the fun

is just starting. There's the carnival, the pony auction—"

"Don't forget the pony parade," Sarah cut in excitedly. "That comes first."

"When is the pony parade?" Yuki asked.

"In about an hour," Sarah said. "First the swimming ponies take a rest. Then the salt-water cowboys parade them up Main Street to the carnival grounds."

Hearing about the parade, carnival, and auction made Willa feel better. Chipper and Sarah were right. The pony swim festivities had just begun.

With the boat safely docked, Willa, Sarah, and Yuki squeezed through the crowd on the beach. Mrs. Starling and the boys had stopped to buy fried oysters from a stand, but the girls were too excited to eat.

"Let's find a good spot on Main Street," Willa told Sarah and Yuki as they walked ahead. "So we can see all the ponies."

People were already lining up and down Main Street when the girls reached town. They were lucky to grab a great viewing spot right at the curb.

As they waited for the parade to begin, Yuki asked, "Why are there so many wild ponies on Assateague Island?"

"Nobody knows the real reason," Sarah explained, "but there are a bunch of stories about how the ponies got there."

"My favorite is the one about the old Spanish shipwreck," Willa said.

"A shipwreck?" Yuki asked.

Willa nodded, happy to tell her favorite story. "Hundreds of years ago a Spanish ship sank off the coast of Assateague Island. The boat was carrying ponies."

"Oh, the poor ponies," Yuki gasped. "Did they go down with the ship?"

"Not all of them," Willa said. "According to the story, many ponies swam all the way to Assateague Island."

"That's where they've been ever since," Sarah said, "for hundreds of years."

"So the horses we saw today are the great-great-great-great-grandponies of the shipwreck survivors?" Yuki asked.

"If the story is true," Willa said.

"I wonder if a treasure chest also washed up

from the shipwreck," Sarah said dreamily. "A huge treasure chest filled with gold and diamonds."

"I know how we can find out," Willa said, a playful gleam in her eye.

"How?" Sarah and Yuki asked at the same time.

"Look for ponies wearing tiaras," Willa joked.

Suddenly the clop-clop-clopping sound of hooves could be heard in the near distance. The three girls leaned over to look up the street. Sure enough, a team of saltwater cowboys rode their ponies down Main Street. Behind them trotted a herd of Assateague ponies.

"Here they come," Yuki exclaimed.

As the herd marched by, Willa saw spectacular ponies of all colors: buckskin, bay, chestnut, palomino.

"That's got to be the stallion," Sarah said.

Willa followed Sarah's gaze to a sturdier, more spirited pony in the parade led by two saltwater cowboys.

Suddenly Willa saw another pony—a tinier foal—break away from the herd and slip through the amused crowd.

"Did you see that?" Willa gasped.

Sarah didn't seem as surprised. "It happens every year," she said. "One of the saltwater cowboys will bring her back."

"I want to do it!" Yuki blurted out.

"Do what, Yuki?" Willa asked.

"Find that foal," Yuki said excitedly. "I think it's the same pony that swam toward our boat."

In a flash, Yuki pushed her way through the crowd. Willa and Sarah traded a shrug then squeezed through the crowd after her.

"There she is!" Yuki shouted.

Willa saw some people chase after the foal, but the little runaway with the spindly legs evaded their capture as she scampered back and forth across grassy front lawns.

"Come on," Yuki said. She waved her hand

in the direction of the foal. "I know how to catch her."

Willa and Sarah joined Yuki in the light-hearted chase. Just when the three friends came within a few feet of the foal, she slipped between two houses.

Led by Yuki, the girls darted between the houses too. They found the runaway pony in a backyard nibbling on fresh green grass.

"Gotcha!" Sarah exclaimed.

"Shh!" Yuki said as the pony picked up her head.

The little foal studied Willa, Sarah, and Yuki with curious brown eyes. They were the same eyes Willa had seen from the boat at the pony swim.

"Hey, there," Yuki greeted the pony softly. "Easy . . . easy. . . ."

With a gentle smile Yuki walked slowly to the foal, her arm stretched out. The pony cocked her head, and shaking her dark brown mane, she welcomed Yuki inching closer and closer.

"Wow," Sarah whispered to Willa. "Whatever books she's reading about ponies I want to borrow."

As Willa watched Yuki, it became clear how much she loved the frisky little pony.

"That's a good girl," Yuki said softly. She was about to touch her when—

"There you are," someone said.

The three friends whirled around. Standing behind them was a smiling saltwater cowboy.

"Looks like we've got an escape artist in the bunch." The cowboy chuckled. "Come on, Houdini, let's get you back before the parade passes you by."

He placed a gentle but firm arm around the foal's neck. His other arm rested on her back as he carefully turned her around. The foal didn't buck. Instead, she allowed the cowboy to lead her back between the houses to Main Street.

"Where will she go now?" Yuki asked.

"Where all the other ponies are going," Sarah explained. "To the carnival grounds and the auction."

"The auction," Yuki repeated. "That means the ponies will be bought, right?"

"Some will," Sarah continued. "The others will swim back to Assateague in a few days."

"You were great with that little foal, Yuki," Willa said. "I think she really liked you."

"Her name is Catalina," Yuki said.

Willa turned to Yuki. "You *named* the pony?"

"It's Spanish," Yuki explained. "I think she should be named after her brave pony ancestors that swam from the Spanish shipwreck to Assateague."

"Catalina," Sarah repeated slowly.

"It's a pretty name," Willa said. "Especially for a pony."

"Speaking of ponies," Sarah said. "Let's go back while there are still ponies on Main Street."

"Oh, right," Yuki answered. She practically skipped ahead of Willa and Sarah as they made their way back to the parade.

"Yuki really likes that little foal," Willa whispered to Sarah.

"Maybe a little too much," Sarah whispered back.

As they looked for a new viewing spot, Willa thought about what Sarah said. What did she mean? How can anyone like a pony *too* much?

Chapter 8

ONCE THE PARADE WAS OVER, WILLA AND YUKI started back to Misty Inn.

"See you at the carnival tonight!" Sarah called, heading home to the Starlings'.

"Tell me more about the pony auction, Willa," Yuki said as their feet crunched along a pebbly path. "Why are the ponies brought to Chincoteague to be sold?"

"To control the size of the herd," Willa explained. "Too many ponies on Assateague Island wouldn't be safe or healthy."

"When is the pony auction?" Yuki asked.

"Tomorrow," Willa answered. "The ponies will be corralled for the night on the carnival grounds. In the morning some will be auctioned off to the highest bidders."

Willa stopped to pick a wildflower. As she twirled the stem between her fingers, she said, "Ben and I will be there tomorrow. We got to see our first pony swim. Tomorrow we'll see our first pony auction."

"I'd like to go to the auction too," Yuki said.

"Great," Willa said. "You'll have to ask your mom, you know. But you can sit with Ben and me. Maybe we'll see Catalina."

Yuki shook her head. "I don't want to just see Catalina, Willa," she said. "I want to buy Catalina."

Stunned, Willa dropped the wildflower on the ground. Did she just hear what she thought she heard?

"You want to buy a pony?" Willa asked.

"With my birthday money," Yuki said. "I was going to buy Chincoteague pony souvenirs. Instead I'll buy a real, live Chincoteague pony!"

"Yuki," Willa said. "A real pony costs more than a pony statue or T-shirt. Your mom doesn't even like horses."

"I won't tell my mom until she meets Catalina," Yuki explained. "I know she'll fall in love with her too."

"But, Yuki—"

"We'll get to stay home together and take care of Catalina," Yuki went on excitedly, "instead of going all over the country on Mom's photo shoots."

"What's wrong with going on her photo shoots?" Willa asked.

"Mom is so busy taking pictures that she has no time for me," Yuki explained. "And when she travels on shoots without me, I miss her."

"Sorry, Yuki," Willa said, feeling bad.

"It's okay, Willa," Yuki said with a smile. "I just know having our own pony will keep Mom at home. It'll be great!"

Willa didn't know what else to say as they approached Misty Inn. When Yuki saw Starbuck grazing in the pasture, she raced toward her.

Willa was about to follow when Ben hurried over.

"You've got to come to the porch, Willa," Ben said breathlessly. "I need your help now."

"What happened?" Willa asked.

"Mr. Ross is talking on his phone again," Ben replied. "This time he looks serious."

Willa drew in a deep breath. She was so busy with the pony swim, parade, and Yuki that she had forgotten about the mystery travel critic. But Ben hadn't.

"He doesn't look happy, Willa," Ben insisted, "and if our critic isn't happy, Misty Inn and Mom and Dad won't be happy after we get a stinky review."

"Okay, okay," Willa said. "Let's offer Mr. Ross

some of Dad's lemonade. That always makes guests happy."

"Good idea," Ben said with a thumbs-up.

As they hurried toward the house, Willa asked, "Should we offer Mrs. Iori some lemonade too?"

"I guess we can," Ben said. "But she's not the mystery travel critic."

Willa stared at her brother. *Mr. Fox wasn't the critic and now Mrs. Iori isn't either? How many guests are left?* she wondered.

"How do you know Mrs. Iori isn't a travel critic?" Willa asked.

"Because she's a wildlife photographer for a travel magazine," Ben explained. "She was showing Mom and Dad pictures she took today of Chincoteague birds and flowers."

That is a neat job, Willa thought. "Any

photos of horses?" she asked hopefully.

"Nope," Ben said.

"Well, if Mrs. Iori isn't the one," Willa told Ben, "that leaves us with Mr. Ross."

Willa and Ben climbed up on the porch, where Mr. Ross sat murmuring into his phone. The Greens were there too. New Cat was curled on Ida's lap as the couple swung lazily on the wooden porch swing.

When Mr. Ross saw Willa and Ben, he ended his call and smiled.

"Hi, Mr. Ross," Willa said, smiling too. "It's very hot. Would you like a glass of our dad's cold lemonade?"

"He makes it with fresh-squeezed lemons and honey," Ben piped in. "One hundred percent natural."

"Lemonade sounds great," Mr. Ross agreed. "Thanks."

"We'd love some lemonade too, please!" Mr. Green said cheerily.

"I'll have a sprig of mint, please," Mrs. Green added, "with crushed ice. Your kitchen does have crushed ice, doesn't it?"

"Crushed and cubes," Willa stated. She didn't mind waiting on Ida and Elmer. Even though they weren't the mystery critics, they still were guests at the inn.

Willa and Ben were about to go inside when Mr. Ross said, "Uh . . . excuse me?"

Willa and Ben turned toward him.

"The pony auction is tomorrow, right?" Mr. Ross asked.

"Bright and early," Willa said.

"Good," Mr. Ross said. He raised an eyebrow. "Because I think I need your help."

Willa and Ben traded a sideways glance. What kind of help? And why was the mystery travel critic being so . . . mysterious?

By the time Willa and Ben went to the carnival that night, they had discovered what Mr. Ross meant. He wanted to bid for a pony at the auction, but not just any pony. It had to be a pony a kid would love.

Mom would be at the auction with the other Misty Inn guests, so she had no problem with Willa and Ben helping Mr. Ross. Willa wanted to help, but she was also puzzled.

"If Mr. Ross is a mystery travel critic," Willa told Sarah and Lena, "why would he want to buy a pony?"

Ben had gone off with Chipper to ride the Ferris wheel. Willa and her friends stood in the cotton-candy line. She had not told Sarah or Lena about Yuki wanting to buy a pony too. Willa hoped she had changed her mind by now.

"I know why Mr. Ross wants a pony," Lena said. "He's testing you to see if you go the extra mile for your guests."

The cotton-candy smell got sweeter and stronger as the girls inched toward the stand. Sarah and Lena watched a juggler. Willa looked at the bustling carnival grounds.

Colorful lights on the rides twinkled against the darkening but still-light summer sky. Both kids and adults tried their luck at noisy arcade games while food stands sold everything from seafood snacks to pony swim souvenirs.

Willa was about to look for the pony corral when someone tapped her arm. It was Yuki, holding a bag of popcorn and wearing a glow-in-the-dark necklace.

"Hi, Yuki," Willa said. "I didn't see you and your mom at dinner."

Yuki pulled Willa away from the line. "My mom wanted to go out for dinner," she said. "But that's not the problem."

"There's a problem?" Willa asked. "What?"

She could see Mrs. Iori in the distance taking pictures of the festivities.

"Mom wants to go to the mainland tomorrow," Yuki complained. "She wants to get away from the crowds."

Yuki's shoulders drooped. "We're leaving so early that I can't go to the pony auction."

Willa didn't want to admit it, but she was a bit relieved. Yuki wouldn't be able to buy Catalina anyway.

"It's okay, Yuki," Willa said. "I know Catalina will get a great home—"

"With me," Yuki cut in. "Willa, will you bid for Catalina for me tomorrow?"

Willa stared at Yuki. "Me? Yuki, I can't do that. I'm too young."

"Sure, you can," Yuki said with a smile. "Just don't be nervous. You'll be awesome."

Willa's heart pounded inside her chest. Yuki really wasn't kidding about buying Catalina.

"I told you," Willa said, "ponies are expensive—"

"I have fifty whole dollars in birthday money," Yuki interrupted proudly. "That ought to do it."

"Fifty dollars?" Willa cried. Ponies at the auction went for *thousands* of dollars. She couldn't believe how unrealistic Yuki was being. Willa was about to explain that when Yuki hurried back to her mom.

"Thanks, Willa!" Yuki called over her shoulder. "Just keep Catalina in your barn until I get back."

"Oh, boy," Willa groaned under her breath. She was joined by Sarah and Lena, cones of cotton candy in their hands.

"I hope you like blue," Sarah said, handing Willa a cone. "Was that just Yuki?"

"What did she want?" Lena asked.

"Just something," Willa muttered, pulling a wad of sticky cotton candy from the cone. "Something impossible!"

Chapter 9

"WHAT ARE YOU GOING TO TELL YUKI, WILLA?" Ben asked. "You can hardly even buy a saddle for fifty dollars."

Willa took a long sip from her water bottle. It was early morning, but the sun was already strong. She and Ben sat in canvas chairs outside the fence of the pony corral.

"I've got to tell Yuki the truth," Willa said.

"That someone with more than fifty dollars bought Catalina."

Willa had told Ben, Sarah, Chipper, and Lena about Yuki's plan at the carnival last night. She had wanted to talk to Yuki after she got home, but the Ioris had gone to bed early. When Willa went downstairs for breakfast the next morning, they had already left for the mainland.

"We have much bigger things to worry about today, Willa," Ben said. "We have to make sure our mystery travel critic gets the pony he wants."

Willa glanced at the empty chair waiting for Mr. Ross. A few chairs away sat Mom and other Misty Inn guests. Mom had done a good job telling everyone to wear hats and sunglasses.

Just then Willa saw Mr. Ross squeezing through the crowd. He smiled at Willa and Ben as he sat in his chair. They watched as Mr. Ross slipped his briefcase underneath.

"I was just talking to your grandpa Reed," Mr. Ross said. "He told me that if I buy a pony today, he'll drive it back to the mainland in his trailer."

Mr. Ross grinned as he went on. "Last night your parents told me I can keep the new pony in your barn until I take it home."

Ben grinned. "Misty Inn aims to please, sir."

Ben was so over the top, Willa had to laugh to herself. But she was glad Mom and Dad agreed to house the pony in their barn. "Since Buttercup is at the Starlings'," she told Ben and Mr. Ross, "the new pony will keep Starbuck company."

"I hope you don't mind if I ask you some pony questions before the auction," Mr. Ross said, putting on his sunglasses. "For starters, what makes a Chincoteague pony special?"

Willa was happy to answer that question. "A Chincoteague pony is smaller, more compact, and sometimes shaggier than others," she explained. "They're usually as sweet as puppy dogs too."

"And they get along great with kids," Ben added. "As you can see, we are kids so we should know."

"Perfect!" Mr. Ross said. "There's one kid I know who will love having her own Chincoteague pony." Mr. Ross held up his phone. On it was a picture of a smiling girl with a missing front tooth, short hair, and big green eyes.

"This is my niece, Taylor," Mr. Ross explained. "She had a rough year being sick, but she's fine now. I'm getting her a pony for her ninth birthday."

"Where does Taylor live?" Ben asked.

"Taylor and her family live in Virginia," Mr. Ross replied. "Not too far from me."

"Do they have a stable?" Willa asked.

"No, but Taylor's grandparents do," Mr. Ross explained. "She'll get to see her new pony almost every day."

"Cool," Willa said. Taylor's grandparents sounded just like Grandma Edna and Grandpa Reed.

"Thanks for explaining the Chincoteague ponies," Mr. Ross said. "You've been a big help."

Ben grinned. "Remember to write that in your review—"

Ben clapped a hand over his mouth. But it was too late. . . .

"What review?" Mr. Ross asked.

Willa rolled her eyes at Ben. Busted!

"We heard a mystery travel critic is staying at Misty Inn," Willa told Mr. Ross. "We deduced it was you. Is it?"

Mr. Ross stared at Willa and Ben, and then laughed. "I wish I had such an adventurous job. I'm a fifth-grade teacher, which actually can be adventurous at times."

"A *teacher*?" Ben said.

"Really?" Willa asked.

"Really." Mr. Ross chuckled. "But don't worry. I won't give you homework."

Willa believed Mr. Ross's story about his niece. She also believed he was a teacher and not a mystery travel critic. But it seemed Ben still had to be sold.

"If you're a teacher, why were your phone calls so serious?" Ben asked. "And why do you need a briefcase? It's summer and most teachers are on vacation."

"Those calls were to my sister about the

pony," Mr. Ross said. He pointed down to his briefcase and added, "I brought papers for identification—just in case I need them to buy a pony."

Ben nodded, and Willa smiled at Mr. Ross. "You're a good uncle for buying Taylor a pony. And I'm glad she's better."

Suddenly—

"Welcome, folks." The auctioneer's voice boomed from his stand. "It's a fine day for a pony auction!"

"Here we go," Willa said excitedly.

The first pony, a little pinto colt, was led into the corral by two saltwater cowboys. The auctioneer spoke so fast, it made Willa giggle.

"Three hundred dollars—three hundred on the left, do I hear three hundred fifty?

Three hundred fifty. Three hundred fifty to Eddie. . . . Do I hear four hundred? Four hundred, four hundred. . . ."

Hands and fingers were raised and bid spotters pointed them out. Willa looked over at Mr. Ross, his hands at his sides.

"Aren't you going to bid?" Willa asked. "That pony seems to have a gentle nature."

"He is nice," Mr. Ross agreed, "but something tells me he's not right for Taylor."

The bidding went up to two thousand dollars until the auctioneer shouted, "Do I hear two thousand three hundred? . . . Anyone? . . . Two thousand three hundred—sold to the woman in the orange Orioles cap!"

Cheers rose as a woman in the ball cap jumped up waving her arms. As the little pony was led out of the corral, Willa hoped he would have a good home.

"Maybe the next pony will be the one," Willa told Mr. Ross. But when Willa looked back at the corral, she gulped. The next pony up was—

"Catalina!" Willa whispered. "Ben, it's her!"

What happened next caused the crowd to roar with laughter. Catalina broke away from the cowboys and began scampering around the ring.

"She did it again!" Willa gasped. "She escaped."

The cowboys had no luck catching Catalina. She finally stopped to nibble some grass growing along the fence. That's when the cowboys took hold.

"Looks like we've got a little firecracker,

folks!" the auctioneer boomed to the laughing crowd. "And a mighty cute one too!"

Willa glanced over at Mr. Ross, who was grinning and leaning forward. What if *Mr. Ross* bought Catalina? She'd be brought back to Misty Inn. Yuki would see Catalina and think she was hers. Willa would have to tell Yuki sooner or later, but Yuki seeing Catalina would make it much, much worse. Willa had to do something. Fast.

"Mr. Ross?" Willa said quickly. "That pony is very, very frisky. She's probably too lively for Taylor."

"You've never met Taylor." Mr. Ross chuckled. "Now that she's well, she's a bundle of energy, just like that foal."

Mr. Ross stood to get a closer look at Catalina.

Willa grabbed Ben's arm. "Ben, we can't let Mr. Ross buy Catalina," she hissed.

"Why not?" Ben whispered.

"Yuki will see her and get upset," Willa said. "Just do whatever you can to stop him."

Ben wrinkled a puzzled nose. "Okay, I'll try."

As the bidding began, Catalina stayed calm, turning her head from time to time to the crowd.

"We'll start with two hundred dollars—do I hear two hundred dollars?" the auctioneer boomed.

Willa was relieved the bidding started higher than fifty. But her worries weren't over yet.

"Three hundred fifty . . . three hundred fifty. . . . Do I hear four hundred?"

Mr. Ross raised his finger. He kept raising

his finger as the bids for Catalina went up to eight hundred dollars.

"Do I hear nine hundred? Nine hundred?"

"Look!" Ben shouted. "They're bringing in a giraffe."

"A giraffe?" Mr. Ross asked, looking around. "Where?"

Ben finally shook his head. "It's just a pony with a long neck. Sorry."

"Nice try," Willa whispered to Ben.

Willa chewed on her thumbnail as the bidding went past one thousand dollars. Then one thousand five hundred. Then—

"Two thousand!" the auctioneer shouted. He swung around, pointing straight at Mr. Ross. "Sold to the man in the straw fedora!"

Mr. Ross leaped to his feet and cheered for

his niece's new pony. Willa was happy that Taylor would be getting her own pony. But how would she explain it to Yuki?

Yuki had her heart set—no matter how ridiculous it seemed—on Catalina. And not going on any more photography trips with her mother.

"I'd better find your grandfather to help me out," Mr. Ross told Willa and Ben. "And see if he's ready to head back to the inn."

Willa wanted to tell Mr. Ross that the foal's name was Catalina but decided not to. Catalina was the name Yuki had given her. And the pony wasn't Yuki's, at least not anymore.

After Grandpa Reed came over, Mr. Ross left to fill out some papers. Willa and Ben watched as Grandpa Reed loaded Catalina into his trailer. She seemed tuckered out after so much running around.

"Mr. Ross said he'll meet us at the inn," Grandpa Reed said, carefully closing the trailer door. "In the meantime, let's get this little spitfire to a stall."

Willa and Ben rode in the backseat of Grandpa Reed's truck as it rambled back to Misty Inn.

"How are you going to keep Yuki from seeing Catalina, Willa?" Ben spoke quietly so Grandpa wouldn't overhear.

"I don't know, Ben," Willa admitted. "I'm hoping Yuki will get back too late today to see Catalina going into the barn."

Willa didn't want to think about tomorrow— she'd worry about that when the time came.

Once at the inn Grandpa Reed opened the trailer and the foal scampered out. Willa and Ben held her tightly as Grandpa Reed slipped a newly bought harness around her head.

"What next, Grandpa?" Ben asked.

"For me?" Grandpa Reed asked. "A cold glass of your dad's iced tea would be nice."

"I'll help you get it," Ben offered.

Grandpa Reed turned to Willa. "Will you be okay bringing the pony to the barn?"

"Sure, Grandpa," Willa said, holding the harness. "I'll give her some fresh water and hay, too."

As Willa walked Catalina toward the barn, she couldn't wait to introduce her to Starbuck.

"Starbuck is from Assateague Island too, Catalina," Willa told the foal. "So you have a lot in common."

Suddenly—

"Willa!"

Willa glanced back. Running toward her with a big smile on her face was Yuki!

"You got her. You got Catalina!" Yuki shouted happily. "I knew you could do it, Willa."

Yuki reached Catalina and wrapped both arms around her neck. "I told Mom I wanted to get back early, and I'm glad I did!" she said. "Thanks, Willa—now Catalina is my pony at last."

Willa held the harness as Yuki buried her face in Catalina's soft coat. How could she tell Yuki the truth? How could she not? She truly had no choice.

"Yuki," Willa began gently, "Catalina was

bought at the auction today . . . but she's not your pony."

Yuki looked at Willa. She was shocked.

"Not my pony?" Yuki asked slowly. "What do you mean she's not my pony?"

Chapter 10

WILLA ALMOST STARTED TO CRY. BUT, INSTEAD, she took one deep breath, then another, and finally spoke.

"I couldn't buy Catalina, Yuki," Willa explained. "But a very nice man did buy her for his niece. Her name is Taylor."

Yuki stared at Willa. Now her eyes were filling with tears. "Catalina can't go to someone else," she cried. "I named her!"

"I know you did," Willa said. "But now Taylor will love her too. Her grandparents have a farm just like mine do."

"But I always wanted a horse," Yuki insisted. "You knew that."

"Horses are great," Willa agreed. "They're also hard work. You have to water, feed, and groom them more than once a day. And muck their stall, which can be gross sometimes."

Catalina tossed her mane as if to agree.

"I don't have a stall," Yuki admitted with a sigh. "We live in an apartment building."

"I used to live in an apartment too, Yuki, in Chicago," Willa said. "There was no way I could ever have had my own pony there."

Willa patted Catalina's withers with a smile.

"Ponies need exercise, too. And this little pony is going to need a ton of exercise."

Yuki sniffed back a chuckle. "That's for sure," she said. "But what will I do without my own pony? I can't just read about them all the time."

Willa didn't know how to help Yuki, until something suddenly clicked. . . .

"Yuki?" Willa asked. "Did you ever ride a horse?"

"Does a carousel count?" Yuki asked glumly. "My mom would never let me ride a real horse. She is always too nervous I'll get hurt or grow too attached to one. And there's a riding academy right in our neighborhood."

There is? Suddenly Willa had a pretty good idea how she could help.

"Yuki, let's put Catalina in a stall and feed her," Willa suggested. "Then let's go talk to your mom."

"About what?" Yuki asked.

Willa smiled as she turned Catalina toward the barn. "You'll see," she said.

Starbuck seemed over the moon to have a brand-new roomie. She whinnied at the first sight of Catalina as Willa led her inside the barn.

Yuki forced a smile as she helped Willa feed and water Catalina. Willa knew it must have been hard for her, knowing that Catalina would belong to someone else.

The moment they got back to the house, Willa shared her plan with Dad, Grandpa Reed, and—most important—Mrs. Iori and Yuki.

"Riding lessons? For Yuki?" Mrs. Iori exclaimed.

"Oh my gosh, yes!" Yuki said upon hearing Willa's idea. "Can I, Mom? *Please?*"

Mrs. Iori had been showing her portfolio of nature photographs to Grandpa Reed on the porch. She shook her head and said, "You know how I feel about horses, Yuki. And how would you go with me on photo shoots when you're busy with riding lessons?"

"That's just it, Mom," Yuki said. "Taking pictures makes you happy, but riding horses will make me happy. And while you watch me take my lessons, we'll be together."

"Who knows, Mrs. Iori?" Willa piped in. "You might want to take riding lessons yourself."

Mrs. Iori stared at Willa. "Riding lessons?

Me?" She laughed. "I wouldn't last three minutes on a horse."

"You might surprise yourself, Andrea," Dad said, pouring Grandpa a fresh glass of iced tea.

"As a matter of fact," Grandpa Reed said, "I know just the place for you and Yuki to take your first lesson."

Willa knew too. "Miller Farm," she stated. "Grandma Edna isn't just a super vet, she's a great riding instructor, too."

"Mom? Please?" Yuki asked.

Willa held her breath, waiting for the answer. Finally Mrs. Iori shrugged and said, "Why not? Maybe I can take some pictures of the animals at the farm."

"And maybe ride one of our biggest animals,"

Grandpa Reed said with a grin. "A nice, gentle horse."

Yuki smiled from ear to ear. She still didn't have Catalina but was getting the next best thing—a chance to be around ponies and ride them too.

Mrs. Iori stood up, tucking her portfolio under her arm. "Okay, Yuki, if we're going to be up close and personal with horses, we'd better change into something rugged," she said. "I still can't believe I'm doing this."

"Me neither, Mom." Yuki giggled. She followed her mother into Misty Inn but not before glancing back at Willa and mouthing, "Thanks."

"You're welcome," Willa mouthed back. She was about to hug Grandpa Reed when Ben stepped out the door.

"I just saw Yuki and she looked happy," Ben asked. "Didn't you tell her about Catalina?"

Willa had just started to explain when Ida and Elmer Green came outside.

"That iced tea looks excellent," Ida declared. She turned to Dad and asked, "Do you make it the same way you did at the Empress Hotel?"

Dad stared at Ida and Elmer. "How did you know I worked at the Empress Hotel in Chicago?" he asked.

Elmer frowned at Ida. "Congratulations, dear," he said. "You just blew our cover."

"Cover?" Dad asked. "What do you mean?"

"Our real names are Roy and Lydia Davis," Elmer explained.

"Roy and Lydia Davis?" Dad gasped. "The travel writers for *Trekking Good* magazine?"

Willa and Ben stared at Elmer and Ida—now Roy and Lydia. *They* were the mystery travel critics? No way!

"How come I didn't recognize you?" Dad asked. "You probably ate at more restaurants I cooked for."

"We're masters of disguises, Eric," Roy explained. "Mostly when we work in the city."

"Roy's right," Lydia joked. "We're actually twenty-five-year-old hipsters."

Dad still looked surprised as he poured two more glasses of iced tea. But no one was as surprised as Willa and Ben.

"So the Greens—I mean Davises—are the mystery travel critics," Ben whispered. "Do you think they like Misty Inn and Family Farm?"

Willa watched the Davises happily sip iced

tea on the porch swing. "I think so," she whispered back.

Now, if only Mrs. Iori would like the horses at Miller Farm.

Later that day Willa's wish would come true. After snapping pictures of the ponies at Miller Farm, Mrs. Iori took a special liking to a gray pinto named Colette. After a little coaxing, Mrs. Iori climbed into the saddle and let Grandma Edna walk her slowly around the ring.

When the ride was over, Mrs. Iori dismounted with a smile. "That was actually fun," she announced. "Maybe Yuki and I *will* take riding lessons back home."

"Yes," Yuki cheered under her breath.

Then it was Yuki's turn to ride. When she

saw Jake, a huge draft horse, she insisted on riding him. With the help of Grandma Edna, Yuki rode the gentle giant around the ring— even trotted!

Yuki did so well on Jake that the next day she rode another gentle pony. She rode Starbuck.

"Is it true, Willa?" Yuki asked from the saddle

as Willa led Starbuck toward the beach. "I heard Catalina is keeping her name."

"It's totally true," Willa said, looking up at Yuki. "Mr. Ross thinks Taylor will love the name Catalina."

Yuki remained silent for a few seconds. She then nodded her head and said, "That's good. Maybe Taylor will learn about Catalina's brave Spanish ancestors, too."

When Willa, Yuki, and Starbuck reached the beach, it was filled with people ready to watch the pony swim. But this time the remaining ponies would be swimming back to Assateague Island, their old home.

Willa leaned her cheek against Starbuck's as they watched saltwater cowboys guide a herd through the white foamy waves. The pony swim festivities on Chincoteague Island would soon be over. But when Willa thought of next summer, she smiled.

On the exact same week next year, the ponies would return to Chincoteague. And if Willa was lucky, so would her new friend Yuki.